Jack and the Beanstalk

Jack and the Beanstalk

Illustrated by MATT FAULKNER

SCHOLASTIC INC.

New York   Toronto   London   Auckland   Sydney

In memory of
Tiki, Duke and Maggie
—M.F.

ISBN 0-590-40164-5

Text copyright © 1965 by Scholastic Books, Inc.
Illustrations copyright © 1986 by Matt Faulkner.
All rights reserved. Published by Scholastic Inc.
Art direction/design by Diana Hrisinko.

12 11 10 9 8 7 6 5 4 3 2 1   4   6 7 8 9/8 0 1/9

ONCE UPON A TIME
there was a poor old woman.
She had a son named Jack.

She had a cow named Milky White.
But that was all she had.

Every day the cow gave milk. And every day the old woman said to Jack, "Sell the milk and bring home the money." And he did. And that was all the money they had.

One morning the cow did not give milk.
"We must sell the cow," said Jack.
"Then take the cow," said the old woman, "and bring home some money."
So Jack took Milky White, and off they went.

Soon they met an old man.

"Good morning," said the old man. "That is a fine cow you have. Do you want to sell her?"

"Yes," said Jack. "Do you want to buy her?"

"Yes," said the old man.

"How much money will you give me?" said Jack.

"I have something better than money," said the old man.

"What is better than money?" said Jack.

"Look," said the old man.

"Beans!" said Jack.

"Yes," said the old man. "Give me your cow, and I will give you five beans."

"I don't want your beans," said Jack.

Heifers
BOUGHT AND SOLD

"But these beans are magic beans," said the old man. "Put them in the ground. Tomorrow they will grow up to the sky."

"Will they?" said Jack.

"They will," said the old man. "If they don't, I will give your cow back to you."

So the man took the cow. And Jack took the beans. He ran all the way home.

"Mother, Mother! See what I got for
the cow!" said Jack.
"Good!" said his mother. "Give me the money."
Jack showed her the beans.
"Beans!" said his mother.
"They are magic beans," said Jack.

11

"Did you sell our cow for five beans? You fool!" said his mother.

"Take that! Take that! Take that!"

Then she took the beans and threw them out of the window.

12

Jack went to bed without any supper.
So did his mother. There was no money.
There was nothing to eat.

Poor Mother! Jack thought.
Poor me!
    At last he fell asleep.

When Jack woke up, the room looked funny.
The sun was shining in one window.
But the other window was full of green leaves.

Jack ran to the window. And what do you
think he saw?

He saw a big beanstalk. The beanstalk
went up and up and up.
It went right up to the sky!

14

"They ARE magic beans!" said Jack.
"And this is a magic beanstalk."
He jumped onto the beanstalk.

15

And he climbed
and
he climbed
and he climbed
and he climbed.

At last he came to the sky. He saw a long road. The road went on and on and on. So Jack walked and walked and walked.

He came to a great big tall house. In front of the house
was a great big tall woman.

"Good morning," said Jack. "Please, can you give me some breakfast?"

"So you would like to eat breakfast," said the woman.

"Well, I know someone who would like to eat YOU for breakfast," she said. "My man is a giant. He likes to eat fresh boys on toast. And I hear him coming right now."

Thump. Thump. Thump.

"Please hide me," said Jack.

The woman was sorry for Jack. So she said, "Quick! jump in here."

And Jack jumped into the oven – just in time.
In came the giant.

"Ah! what's this I smell?" he said.
"Fee fi fo fum
I smell the blood of an Englishman.
Be he alive or be he dead,
I'll grind his bones to make my bread."
"Oh no, dear," said the giant's wife. "I think you can still smell the little boy you ate yesterday. Now don't be silly. Sit down and eat your breakfast."

Jack looked through a crack in the oven door. He watched the giant.

The giant ate his breakfast. Then he took out two bags of gold and began to count the gold.

At last the giant began to get sleepy. His head began to nod. And he began to snore. He snored so loud, the house began to shake.

Then Jack jumped out of the oven.

He grabbed a bag of gold, and he ran and he ran until he came to the beanstalk.

The bag of gold was so heavy, Jack let it fall.
It fell down
      down
         down
into his mother's garden.

Then Jack climbed down
and climbed down.
And at last he was home.

"Mother! Mother!" Jack called. "Look at this!"
And he showed her the bag full of gold.
For a long time Jack and his mother
had plenty of money.

But one day all the money was gone.
"Well," said Jack to his mother. "I will
try my luck again."

So he got onto the beanstalk, and he climbed and
he climbed and he climbed
   and he climbed.
   At last he came to the road again.

And he found the great big tall house again. And in front of the house was the great big tall woman again.

"Good morning," said Jack, bold as brass. "Please, can you give me some breakfast?"

"You're the same boy who came here before!" said the great big tall woman.

"Maybe you can tell me what happened to the bag of gold the giant lost that day."

"Maybe I can," said Jack. "But I am so hungry, I can't talk."

"Then I'll give you something to eat," said the woman.

All at once –
thump thump thump.
They heard the giant coming.
    The woman hid Jack in the
oven. And everything happened
as it did before.
    The giant said, "Fee fi fo fum."
His wife said, "Don't be silly."
The giant ate his breakfast.

After breakfast, he said,
"Wife, bring the hen that lays
the golden eggs."
Then the giant said to the hen,
"Lay." And the hen laid
an egg all of gold.

At last the giant began to get sleepy.
His head began to nod.
And he began to snore.
He snored so loud,
the house began to shake.

Jack jumped out of the oven. He grabbed the hen and off he ran. But the hen made a noise, and the giant woke up.

Jack heard the giant call, "Wife, wife, what did you do with my golden hen?"

But that was all Jack heard. He ran to the beanstalk and climbed down like a house-on-fire.

"Mother! Mother!" Jack called.
"Look at this."
    Jack showed his mother the hen.

    "Lay," said Jack.
    The hen laid an egg all of gold.
    Every time Jack said, "Lay,"
the hen laid
a golden egg.

One day Jack said to his mother,
"Maybe the giant has more things.
I am going to try my luck again."
Jack got onto the beanstalk
and he climbed
and he climbed
and he climbed
and he climbed.

At last he got to the top.

But this time Jack did not go right to the giant's door.
This time he hid behind a bush. He saw the giant's wife
go down the road to get some water.
Jack crept into the house and
climbed into a big pot.

Soon he heard thump thump thump. The giant and his wife came in.
"Fee fi fo fum
I smell the blood of an Englishman," the giant said.
"Do you, my dear?" said the giant's wife. "Well, if it is that rascal Jack you smell, he will be in the oven. That is where he likes to hide."

They both ran to the oven.
The giant opened the door.
But Jack wasn't there,
thank goodness!

"Oh," said the giant's wife, "there you go again! I think you must be smelling the little boy you ate yesterday."

"Now don't be silly. Eat your breakfast."

The giant sat down to eat. He kept jumping up to look for Jack. But he did not look in the big pot, thank goodness!

After breakfast, the giant said, "Wife, bring me my golden harp."

She brought the harp and put it on the table.
"Sing," said the giant.
And the golden harp sang.
At last the giant began to get sleepy.
His head began to nod.
And he began to snore.
He snored so loud, the
house began to shake.

Then Jack crept out of the pot. He was as
quiet as a mouse. He crept to the table.
He climbed up the table leg.
He grabbed the harp. Then he
climbed down and began to run.

But the harp called out, "Master! Master!"
The giant woke up.

He was just in time to see Jack running off with his harp.

Jack ran as fast as he could. The giant came running after him.

Then Jack got onto the beanstalk and began to climb
    down
        down
            down.

The giant stopped. He was afraid to climb down the beanstalk.

But the harp cried out once more, "Master! Master!"

43

So the giant jumped onto the beanstalk. He began climbing down faster and faster.
But Jack was ahead of him.
"Mother! Mother!" Jack called.
"Bring me the ax! Bring me the ax!"

Jack's mother came running with the ax.
She saw the giant's big feet.
She was so frightened,
she could not move.

But Jack jumped down.
He grabbed the ax.
He gave a chop at
the beanstalk.

The giant felt the beanstalk shaking.
Then Jack gave another chop with the ax.
The beanstalk fell to the ground,
and the giant fell with it.
And that was the end of the giant.

Then Jack showed his mother
the golden harp.

People paid money to hear the harp sing. And
every day the hen laid a golden egg.

So Jack and his mother became very rich.
And they lived happily ever after.